Written in the Stars

By Prometheus Susan

Megan
follow your heart
Prometheus
Susan

Prometheus Susan

Copyright 2022© Prometheus Susan

All rights reserved. This book, or any portion thereof, may not be reproduced or used in any manner without the express written permission of the author except for brief quotations used in book reviews.

This book is a work of fiction. The names, characters, places, and incidents are products of the writer's imagination or have been used fictitiously and are not to be construed as real. Any resemblance to persons, living or dead, actual events, locales, or organizations is entirely coincidental.

Table of Contents

CHAPTER 1 ....**5**

CHAPTER 2 ....**8**

CHAPTER 3 ....**11**

CHAPTER 4 ....**14**

CHAPTER 5 ....**17**

CHAPTER 6 ....**20**

CHAPTER 7 ....**23**

CHAPTER 8 ....**26**

CHAPTER 9 ....**30**

CHAPTER 10 ....**34**

CHAPTER 11 ....**38**

CHAPTER 12 ....**42**

CHAPTER 13 ....**45**

CHAPTER 14 ....**48**

CHAPTER 15 ....**52**

CHAPTER 16 ....**55**

CHAPTER 17 ....**58**

CHAPTER 18 ....**62**

CHAPTER 19 .... **66**

CHAPTER 20 .... **69**

CHAPTER 21 .... **73**

CHAPTER 22 .... **76**

CHAPTER 23 .... **79**

CHAPTER 24 .... **82**

CHAPTER 25 .... **85**

ABOUT THE AUTHOR **87**

OTHER TITLES BY PROMETHEUS SUSAN **88**

Chapter 1

She stood on the steps of the courthouse, looking up at the tall building. Why did this building look foreboding? Saturn knew the answer. Lives were changed behind those heavy wooden doors. Once you stepped inside, fate finished what it started. For her, it was the ending of her marriage.

There was some sadness within her over the divorce, but anger won the race with her emotions. Some of the anger was aimed at Stanley, her soon-to-be ex. Most of what she was feeling was with herself. How could she not have seen his cheating sooner? Why had she not been good enough? The biggest one was, why in the hell had she married the ass?

The one thing she was thankful for was they kept separate bank accounts. No joint credit cards, either. His debt was all on his shoulders. Stanley tried to make her pay half of his credit cards. Why should she have to pay for jewelry that went to some other woman? He tried to get half of her savings account. The dumbass even tried for spousal support. He lost those battles thanks to a prenup she had insisted upon.

There had been something about Stanley her parents hadn't liked. They stressed to her the importance of having a prenup. Her savings weren't in the millions, but it was a nice nest egg with her investments. Saturn had done it to put her parents' minds at ease. They had seen Stanley for the snake he was.

The only item she wanted from Stanley in the divorce was half of their condo. He had been the one who wanted to live in that building. She wanted a little bungalow further out of town, with a yard. Regardless, it had been her money that paid for half of what was their home. Everything else they split up. He kept the furniture. Saturn had taken the possessions that were important to her. Any gifts that he gave her, she left behind.

She was ready to put this ordeal behind her. Once the judge's gavel went down, Stanley would be out of her life. Saturn quit her job, prepared to make a fresh start. Put this disaster of a marriage behind her. Who knew that two years ago, saying their vows, that the happily ever after was an illusion?

There was an eerie coldness to the courtroom as she walked in. The hushed whispers between attorney and client. Glares from one party to the next. It was apparent who paired with whom. Saturn ignored Stanley and his attorney as she went to sit with hers.

This divorce could have been settled months ago. Stanley had contested it. Prolonging the inevitable with his lame attempts to either hurt her further or gain more money. A year of her life was spent going back and forth.

The funny part was she had no feelings left for the man she married. Money could be replaced with hard work, but she wasn't about to give it away.

Her case was called, and she took a seat next to her attorney. Saturn listened to Stanley's attorney argue over the fact that her soon-to-be ex-husband would have to change his lifestyle. Her attorney countered with evidence of his infidelities, proof that he could live a prosperous life with what he earned. It was not up to her to provide him with the funds to live beyond his means. That had been one of their ongoing arguments. One of the reasons they were standing in this courtroom.

Chapter 2

Stanley hadn't been concerned with how much she earned when they were dating. Maybe she didn't see it. Some said love was blind. When they met, she had been working a contract job at NASA with her parents. Saturn tried to explain that to him. He heard what he wanted to. After they were married, her contract ended, and she went back to teaching science at the local high school.

To say that her husband was disappointed was an understatement. It had been their first argument. He accused her of misleading him, getting them into debt. Saturn remembered his words clearly. I only married you for your status. Working for NASA is all I was attracted to, not you. You look good on paper to those higher up in my office. Good for a promotion, nothing else.

That was also when he started coming home later. He would make comments about how the condo was a mess, how she needed to lose weight, work out, learn to cook; in other words, be a better woman and wife. Saturn had always been self-confident, but hearing those words made her doubt herself. She had joined a gym, only to hear, Stop wasting my hard-earned money.

No amount of working out is going to change the fact that you are fat and homely.

After what seemed like an eternity, the judge ruled his decision. They were no longer married. Saturn had her freedom. She hadn't taken Stanley's name when they married. Now, she didn't have that constant reminder. Her soul felt lighter as she said goodbye to her attorney and walked out of that courtroom.

She wasn't expecting this blonde woman to grab her arm, yelling at her. "How dare you make me work? Stanley deserves the money for putting up with you. You are lucky he put up with your ugly ass for as long as he did. Alimony should have been for pain and suffering."

Saturn could only guess that this woman was the mistress. She shrugged, pulling her arm away from the offensive woman. "He is all yours, honey."

Saturn left it at that. She did not owe this woman an explanation or an argument. That part of her life was over, time to move on. She held her head high as she walked down those hallways, down the steps. That first breath of fresh air as she cleared the doors smelled fresher, the sun seemed brighter, the usual noise from others, and traffic seemed to be dulled. For those others did not matter in her life anymore. Her life was hers once again to live as she saw fit.

As she climbed into her SUV, she was thankful she traded her little car for something bigger. All of her belongings fit into the back. Saturn had downsized when she moved out. A lot of excess baggage had been lost when she moved out, and today, the rest was gone. All in all, she had lost over two hundred pounds in a matter of minutes, the best damn diet she ever tried.

Chapter 3

Her first stop had been one of her favorite fast-food places. Never again would she eat a salad to please a man. Those days were long gone. If anyone couldn't accept her for who she was, then they could go fuck themselves. Saturn wasn't sure when she lost herself. Once she moved out, her old self was making a comeback. It felt good to not have to be someone that, deep down, you knew you weren't.

Saturn enjoyed her French fries and bacon cheeseburger as she sped up to join the other travelers on the highway. She had two weeks before her new home would be ready. It was a quaint cabin settled across from the forest on an acre of land. Enough for her to plant a garden if she wished, maybe build a gazebo, a fire pit to enjoy the cooler nights. She could see her neighbors' houses from hers on either side. No one was behind her.

It had been a quick trip when she had gone out to the small town of Moonless, Wyoming. There had been an ad on a website looking for a science teacher for their school district. Saturn didn't realize until after she applied and went for the interview that the school district was one school.

She would be teaching science from first grade to twelfth. It was a challenge she was looking forward to. The differences between the grades were astounding, but she loved opening up little ones' minds to the unknown. Seeing them learn something new, when it all clicks in their heads, it's a sight that never got old.

Stanley never understood why she loved teaching over research and development. It wasn't about the money to her. It was making a difference. With children, the difference was more important than any discovery she could ever make. She still did a consultation project with NASA. That was more because it was usually one of her parents' projects she was helping with. It was not a career she wanted full-time.

The first time she saw the cabin, she was in love with it. It had been what she was looking for. Someplace that would be hers, not a house but a home. She could envision herself sitting on the front porch with a hot cup of coffee, watching the sunrise. Being in the kitchen with snow falling outside, baking cookies while a fire blazed in the fireplace.

That was the life she hoped to have when she got married. It was the polar opposite. That was in the past. Now it was her time to have what she wanted out of life. Saturn looked forward to planting flower beds around the front porch, hanging wind chimes, a clothesline to hang out sheets, and the ability to wear leggings without hearing derogatory comments.

If she felt like a sandwich for dinner, there was no one to criticize her for being a lazy ass and not providing a substantial meal. Saturn could spend all Saturday lounging in bed or on the couch watching movies. On a day when the students were a bit hyper, she had the option of coming home and soaking in a hot bath with a glass of wine. She could put her long hair up into a ponytail and not hear how fat her face looked that way. No make-up, not a problem. Her world was open for her to do as she pleased. She was free.

Chapter 4

Saturn mapped out her trip. Her plans were to make stops along the way at places she had never visited before. The first stop was Niagara Falls. She took one of the boat trips, bought a couple of knick-knacks for her new home, and a sweatshirt. Saturn toured the Cave of the Winds, glad she thought to wear sandals. Her sneakers would never have dried if she wore them.

Her road trip took her up through Michigan. When she had been searching for exciting landmarks while planning her move, one place caught her attention, Frankenmuth, Michigan, and it's Christmas store. Saturn was looking forward to having a live Christmas tree, decorating to her heart's delight. Her parents decorated for Christmas and held an annual party. She missed celebrating the holiday.

Stanley despised all holidays. She never understood why. All he ever said was, "They are a waste of time and money. Especially Christmas, where everyone wants a handout in the form of a gift."

Saturn giggled to herself as she sped down the highway. She could celebrate as she saw fit. That thought led her to think about Halloween. Carved pumpkins sitting on each step up to the front door. Fake cobwebs hanging from post to post and orange lights along the railing. She was getting excited about her new home.

She had tried to limit herself in the Christmas store. It wasn't easy. Everywhere you looked, there was something different. Any kind of ornament one could imagine. She found a couple of ones that depicted the Milky Way galaxy. Saturn bought her parents a set as well as herself. Luckily the store offered a shipping service. Once she found that out, her cart became heavier to push.

Then she found the other shops in town. Saturn had been collecting wolf figurines since she received one on her sixteenth birthday. Seemed fitting as she studied the effects of the full moon that wolves were a part of her study. She found garden statues of wolves that she wanted for her flower gardens. At this rate, she would have a porch full of packages by the time she arrived in town.

Her cabin had been empty for a couple of years, according to her realtor. When she bought it, part of the contract was that the sellers would put on a new roof, clean the inside, mow the weeds, replace most of the porch, upgrade the electrical, and remodel the bathroom and kitchen. Saturn thought that was too much. She didn't mind doing a little remodeling when she moved in, but Sable said, "The seller is okay with doing these repairs."

The sellers let her pick out the flooring, countertop, and tiles for the remodeling. She felt guilty, as though she was taking advantage of them. Sable reassured her numerous times, "This is how we do things in small towns." Saturn was excited to see her new home with the changes done.

Her parents were planning on making a trip out to visit her. That was one thing she had always counted on was their support. Her life decisions would have them voicing their concerns, but in the end, when it was a mistake, they were there if she needed them. This move was not a mistake. For the first time since meeting Stanley, this felt right. As though fate was guiding her to Moonless, Wyoming.

Chapter 5

He took over the pack when his dad retired. Dash's sister was mated, expecting their first pup at any time. His parents wanted to spend more time with their grandchild, travel the world while they could. The pack ran like a well-oiled machine. Grievances were handled immediately to avoid a festering confrontation that divided them.

There was one thing he did change. The packhouse was not where he lived. His parents had moved into a smaller house between his and his sister's homes. Dash turned the packhouse into a recreational building with offices for himself, his beta, and the doctor. One location for all to find what they needed. The pack doctor had a more significant area than one room of his home. Both the beta and he had more privacy with having an office there, home someplace else.

This change meant that pack dinners were once a week, not nightly. He had seen too often how hard his mother, along with other females, worked to make dinner for thirty. Dash didn't want that for his mate if he ever found her. He wanted them to have privacy. Enjoy one another without an audience. Not that he didn't think of the pack as family. It was the fact that he wanted to learn about his mate, make mistakes without having advice from everyone.

The cabin on the outskirts of pack land he decided to sell. None of the pack members wanted to live that far away from everyone else. It belonged to a widowed male who had lost his mate in childbirth. The male left the pack to travel the world, giving the pack the deed to the land and house. Dash let his sister, Sable, find a suitable buyer. His stipulation was they would fix up the cabin for whoever bought it.

He hadn't met the new resident of Moonless, Wyoming. His mom interviewed her for their school. Moonless was made up of the pack. All residents were pack, the same as the businesses. Dash knew of a few towns like theirs. It made the pack strong, fruitful. Everyone did what they loved, less conflict. As the pack's Alpha, he was also the mayor. Usually, he was supposed to meet all who moved into town. His dad took his place, as he was busy transforming the packhouse.

All Dash knew was the new science teacher had outstanding credentials. They were lucky to have snagged her. The kids were going to learn so much from her. Their school had been lacking a science teacher for a few years. Science was one of his favorite subjects, especially astronomy. He enjoyed hiking to the top of one of the smaller mountains. There was a flat clearing that was perfect for setting up a telescope. You were high enough above the trees that they didn't block your view, but low enough that it wasn't a challenging hike.

The only problem with the new teacher was that she was human. Once some of the single males found out about that, and they started plotting ways to meet her. Dash understood where they were coming from. Some of them were in their forties, which for a werewolf was not that old. It was the yearning for a mate. A true, fated mate that drove most of them. There got to be a time when you didn't feel complete, like a piece was missing. It was your wolf's other half. He felt it at times. Not like he hadn't had plenty of offers from single she-wolves. He was not settling.

Chapter 6

She stopped at outlet malls that lined the highway on her way. Spending a night or two in a nearby hotel. Saturn knew what colors she picked out for the bathroom and kitchen. On each of her stops, she made purchases for her new home.

None of the dishes from the condo had she brought with her. Stanley had picked them out. She hated them. Her one favorite cast iron skillet, he had pitched a fit about how it looked. At some point, it went missing. The dumbass did not grasp the concept of seasoning with those kinds of skillets. The uglier it looked, the more seasoned it was. Didn't mean it was dirty.

This time she picked out pots, pans, and dishes she liked. Saturn didn't give two shits who made them or if they were fine china or not. If she liked it, she bought it. Who used fine china daily? She had that answer—Stanley. He had always said that was the proper method of serving dinner. Maybe on special occasions, not every day. Her parents were down to earth. Some nights it was paper plates if no one wanted to do dishes.

The one time she bought paper plates, Stanley threw them out. Bitching nonstop. "They are a waste of money. Who do you think we are? This is not some picnic. Are you that stupid to think you could serve me dinner on paper? We can afford the best china. I expect to see china at the dinner table at all times."

Giggling to herself as she bought paper plates, Saturn knew Stanley would never know, but she was taking back who she was in some part of her mind. Thumbing her nose at her ex-husband and his stupid rules. She was going with a coffee theme for her kitchen. She found towels, rugs, and small pictures that would decorate the space nicely. No more would her rooms be sterile and white. They would reflect her personality.

She left most of her clothes in the closet of the condo. They weren't who she was. Saturn liked jeans, leggings, bulky sweaters, printed shirts, hoodies, and t-shirts. She had a few dresses she took. They were a sweatshirt material that was utterly soft and comfortable. A few of them were summer sundresses that could be paired with a cardigan or light jean jacket. She had taken her shoes. There were a couple pairs of boots she would kill over. They were that comfortable.

Most of these malls had clothing stores. She walked through the various shops, picking up what she liked. Moving to Wyoming, she figured the winters were colder. She would need more sweaters. Which led her to throw blankets that were buttery soft. Saturn looked forward to snowy winter nights with a fire blazing, snuggled on the couch with a good book or movie. Cup of coffee or hot cocoa in hand, a plate of homemade cookies by her side.

The more she shopped, the fuller her SUV became. Saturn added candles to the mix. There was something about having candles burning while taking a hot bubble bath that washed away all the day's stresses. Bubble salts were added to her basket. The more she roamed around the bath store, her basket got heavier as she added lotion and shower gel sets. Stanley hated the way the bathroom smelled after she showered. He had said, "You leave a cloud of perfume when you use the bathroom. You know I have a sensitive nose."

The more she thought back to her short marriage to Stanley, the more she saw what an ass he had been. It was all about him. From buying the condo to decorating it, it was all him. How she dressed, acted, once again all about him. Saturn had ceased to be herself. She became what was needed to keep him happy. That was never happening again.

She asked that, when they remodeled the bathroom, to leave the big, clawfoot tub. It would be perfect for soaking in. Saturn was ready to get to her new home. This time on the road gave her time to reflect on the past couple of years. See that, while she had changed to please Stanley, that was reversible. She was coming back into her own. Life was going to be good.

Chapter 7

She had been trying to get pregnant since they started their affair. Heather made appointments with a gynecologist to find a reason for no pregnancy after a year or so. Each doctor had the same answers. "There is no medical condition or reason as to why you are not getting pregnant. Could it be your partner? We need to run some tests on him."

Heather thought over what the doctor asked for. How could she get him to cum into a cup without his knowledge and bring it to the office within twenty minutes? Would her giving him a blow job then spitting it all into a cup alter what they were looking for? She could give him a hand job. That had better potential, except for that time frame. How could they have sex and she run to the office for an exam without raising suspicion? She was resourceful, but there were limits.

That was where she ran into a bit of a problem. Stanley did not know she was off her birth control. Nor did he know she was trying to become pregnant. Heather wasn't stupid. He was a good man, they had a lovely home, a great car, were invited to corporate parties, and he made a decent wage. She was trying to tie him to her for a good eighteen years or more. The problem was her little plan was not working as she hoped.

Her mind ran through all different scenarios of how to deceive him to get what she wanted. If she was not the problem, that left him. Heather had an idea. Maybe his little sperm were not great swimmers. They needed a little push. How hard could it be to give them that little extra burst? She could collect the little swimmers, use a turkey baster to provide them with that extra push, get them closer to the prize.

Stanley asked her to move in with him as they left the courthouse. She had cleaned out the closet his ex-wife had been using. Not a designer label on anything she left behind. It was all garbage. The jewelry she had taken to be appraised. All fake costume jewelry, worth nothing. Heather thought that woman had no class. Finding all of this solidified that.

If you are with a successful man, a woman needs to look the part. He wanted a hot wife or girlfriend on his arm. Not someone who took no interest in how she looked. Heather had seen the ex-wife at court. No highlights in her hair, essential, drab clothing, sneakers, and no make-up. As plain as one could get. She understood why Stanley had been keeping her bed warm while married.

It had been while she was cleaning, snooping, whatever, that she found the life insurance paperwork. From what Heather understood of them, Stanley was still the beneficiary if something accidentally happened to

Saturn. It was for one million dollars. That would make all of her dreams come true. She tucked the papers away in her purse. This would be her project. A pleasant surprise to Stanley when it was completed.

Chapter 8

Saturn pulled up in front of her cabin, shocked at how it looked. It had been power washed, the porch looked completely new, a swing was anchored on one side with rockers on the other. She read the note taped to the front door. Welcome to Moonless, Wyoming. Any questions, give the mayor a call at 307-744-0002. The first day of school is Wednesday as a teacher institute day.

She was taken aback by having the mayor's phone number. That would never happen in a big city. Saturn thought she had a lot to learn about small towns. They did seem more personable. Her culture shock continued when she opened the door. Walking in, a bouquet of wildflowers greeted her on the counter next to a basket filled with muffins and cookies. Way better than fruit was her first thought.

Next to the basket was a package from the school. She opened it to find a set of keys, instructions for each key, a calendar for the year, a schedule of her classes, and class lists of students for each period. Saturn liked how the kids were grouped by grade. Kindergarten was with first graders. Second through fourth, fifth with sixth, seventh with eighth, freshman with sophomores, and junior with seniors. She had six classes throughout the day on some days.

The younger children saw her twice a week. Made sense to her. They needed the beginning of science. Saturn planned on starting them all out on the weather. Since it was still nice outside, they could take their studies out. Even the little ones would benefit from learning about clouds, rain, snow, and storms. She looked over the class lists. Some of the classes had two kids. The most had four. A shock from where she had come from. Her smallest class back where she used to live was twenty-five. This was going to be fun. More hands-on than any place she had taught before.

She walked around her new home. The kitchen came out beautiful. The tan and dark brown tile made the area feel warm. Blended with the tan paint on all the walls, each room flowed into the next. Her furniture had been delivered. She would have to thank whoever set it up for her. Saturn was expecting it to all be in the living room, not set up in the room it belonged in. That was a pleasant surprise.

After her walk-through, she headed outside to start unloading her SUV. Saturn thought ahead and stopped for groceries. Those needed to come in first. The cold items had to be taken care of before anything else. She jumped when voices sounded behind her.

"Hey, welcome to Moonless. Sable told us that you were arriving today and may need a hand. Can we help you get this unloaded? I'm Blake and this is my brother, Jake."

Saturn turned to come face to chest with two of the most gorgeous men she ever laid eyes on. They didn't make men like these in the city. Good-looking men in the city knew they drew the eye of every woman they passed. These two didn't seem like that type.

"Sable mentioned something about sending someone to help me move in. Thank you. I would like your help. I'm Saturn. The new science teacher at the Moonless school."

Blake and Jake had her SUV unloaded by the time she had the groceries put away. She placed the bags or boxes in the rooms where she wanted them. Saturn had them help her rearrange her bedroom. She wanted the bed under the window so that the cool night air would blow over her. It was at this time that her patio set and grill were delivered. Her dad was an expert griller. It was something she missed living with Stanley. He hated barbequed food. She never understood that. Grilled hotdogs were one of the best foods on a hot summer day. A little bit of relish, mustard, and ketchup. Her stomach growled in agreement.

She started unpacking her kitchen items while Blake and Jake worked on her grill and patio set. The patio set was the easier of the two. She swore they had it together in a matter of minutes. Saturn wanted to grill some hotdogs for dinner. She bought a container of potato salad at the store. It wasn't much, but she was willing to share with her helpers. They saved her countless hours. With their help, she would be unpacked by the time she started working. That put her mind at ease. Being settled before the craziness of the start of school would make her life much more pleasant.

Jake was enjoying being around Saturn. There was something about her. "If you ever want to get some fresh eggs or milk the Peter's farm is the place to go. Sam had the best produce. Honey has the best honey. She plants clover for her bees. All of them have stands on Saturday's down main street. When the weather turns cold, they move into the school gym. "

He took a bite of his hotdog. Nothing better than a good grilled dog. Blake liked that Saturn didn't put on airs like some he knew. "The diner in town has been handed down for generations. When it gets cold, the have the best soups. You will have to try their BLT's. They don't skimp on the bacon. You must stop at Donna's bakery. Her bear claws are the best. Get there early, they sell out fast. If someone is making a trip to one of the big stores in the city. They will ask if you need anything. That's how it is here in Moonless."

Saturn enjoyed sharing her meal with Blake and Jake. She learned a little about the town. Most of the residents had lived there all their life. The businesses are handed down from generation to generation. They had helped her clean up from dinner, said their goodbyes. She closed the front door, leaning against the door as she looked at her new home. A fresh beginning that she had been looking for, a new start in a new place.

Chapter 9

Saturn spent the days before school started unpacking. Dire and Tala had stopped by with a container of chicken and dumplings, introducing themselves to her as well as welcoming her to town. She had found out that Dire was the retired mayor. It was their son, Dash, that was the current one. It was a pleasant visit with the two of them. The best chicken and dumplings that she ever had.

What she found amusing was how she mentioned needing firewood, or how she wanted to get one of those outdoor firepits. Within a few hours after Dire and Tala left, there was a knock on her front door. Blake and Jake stood there with a truckload of firewood. Behind them came Mark and Henry with one of those outdoor firepits. They had introduced themselves as the sheriff deputies of Moonless. Saturn was stunned as they went to work putting it together while the wood was stacked in the wood carrier on the side of the cabin.

This did not happen in a big city. She was happy she chose to move to a small town out west. Some would not like the closeness of knowing everyone in town. Or how those that didn't know you came and did things for you without asking. Saturn didn't have a problem with any of it. If anything, it warmed her heart to feel like a part of the community. To be accepted in a new place felt good.

Mark built a fire outside. Henry pulled out the makings for s'mores. They sat around the fire, roasting the leftover hotdogs that she had, making s'mores while enjoying a cold beer. What she noticed the most with these men was their manners. Not one of them had used any pick-up lines on her. They were genuine in their offering of help as a friend.

This was one more point where she and Stanley had not gotten along while they were together. He had always said, "Men cannot be friends with a woman. It's always about sex. A woman sees a man for what he can do for her. It's either money or babies."

Saturn thought he was an idiot when he said that, still did. She couldn't stop the giggles that erupted. Even if it earned her raised eyebrows from the four guys sitting around the fire.

Attempting to catch her breath from giggling as hard as she was, Saturn had to explain, "I'm not laughing at you. It's more that I'm laughing at something my ex-husband used to say. He would say men and women cannot be friends. Women were after two things from any man. Either money or babies. I thought about that and realized his girlfriend fit that perfectly. She got mad at me when the divorce was final at the courthouse because he didn't get more money. I was wondering if she was pregnant yet. Which made me giggle. It would serve him right."

Blake shrugged right along with the rest of them. Each of them sought out the new female that moved into town with hopes that she was their mate. Saturn wasn't meant for any of them, but she was a mate to a wolf. He had his hunch on who it was. They all did. That meeting would happen when fate decided it was time. They planned on looking out for her. Become the big brother that she needed. "Sounds like that ex was a fool. One, he let you go; two, cheated on you; three, has no clue about what being a friend means. Here's the difference, sweetie. Our dads taught us how to treat a female properly. Don't get me wrong, some women are after only that, but you cannot judge one because of another's actions."

She ended up telling them all about her marriage to Stanley. How he would berate her over any little thing. His derogatory words whenever he got a chance. How long the divorce had taken to be granted. His fighting over money, her money. It was something that she had not spoken to anyone about, not even her parents. Saturn swore she heard growls but didn't see any animals nearby. She chalked it up to the beer.

Blake looked between Jake, Mark, and Henry. Each of them were trying to control their wolves. It was not an easy task with what she told them. He could tell she hadn't spoken of this before now. Some men were dumbasses, not seeing the beauty that was sitting before them. Saturn was beautiful inside and out. She had a kind soul. Blake knew the rest of them would talk when they got back home. He could see it written across his pack mate's faces that they were thinking the same thing that he was. If this ex fought the divorce, did not see where he was treated fairly, he could pose a problem. Would this fucker hunt her down to prove a point? Time would tell, but meanwhile, they would keep a protective eye on their new friend.

Chapter 10

The school year started without a problem. Saturn enjoyed each of the classes she taught. The children were full of energy and questions. Where did she come from? Why was she single? For most of those, she redirected the kids to the subject at hand. They were curious, which she understood. She was new in town.

Time seemed to pass quickly. The first week turned into a month. Saturn was settled into her new life. She had a schedule. Mornings she enjoyed her cup of coffee sitting out on her front porch, listening to the birds. She usually had a muffin for breakfast as she was making her lunch. The school day flew by.

When she got home, some days, she grilled something easy. Other times she cooked ramen. A few times, she stopped at the diner in town and had dinner. Saturn never could figure out how when she stopped, as soon as she was seated, Blake, Jake, Mark, or Henry would show up to keep her company, eating with her. One of those four seemed too always be around. It was comforting.

She felt alone married to Stanley. Even when they went to a party or function, he was off doing whatever he did, leaving her to fend for herself. The more she thought about it, the more that she realized something. He was hardly home when she was. If they were together, they argued, or he was busy making her feel inadequate. Saturn had spent more time alone while married than being single.

While they were studying the weather, she made sugar cookies in the shape of clouds or lightning bolts. The kids loved having a treat while learning. She enjoyed the fact that she could do this for her students and others. Never failed when she was baking that she had visitors at her door. It was comical how grown men would barter for a cookie. Life was good. She had a job that she loved. A home that was hers. Saturn was happier than she had been in a few years.

***

He had been hearing nothing but good things about the new resident to Moonless. Dash wished his schedule would lighten up a little so that he could meet her. Blake, Jake, Mark, and Henry were his best friends. They had all grown up together, raised hell at times. Blake and Jake were his seconds in command or betas. Mark and Henry were his marshals, also the town's sheriffs.

One of the four clued him in when Saturn was at the diner. It never failed that as soon as he was attempting to leave to casually pop in, Scarlett had some life-threatening problem that needed to be handled. Not once was it as severe as she made it out to be. The she-wolf was giving him a headache. Dash was not interested in her romantically, never had been, never would be. The problem was, she thought with persistence, she could wear down his resolve. What Scarlett didn't know, his wolf couldn't stand the way she smelled.

Most of the pack avoided her like the plague. Scarlett wasn't an outcast within the pack. She was included in the monthly runs, weekly dinners. Her attitude towards being self-reliant put most off. The damsel in distress did not fare well with wolves. Rude comments said under her breath that, with their enhanced hearing, all could hear. She brought it upon herself by chasing after every single male, putting finding a mate over everything else. Even if that mate did not belong to her. Not being welcoming to new mates. It was a fine line with her. She was close to being asked to leave the pack.

It had to be a mutual agreement to become mates outside of what fate decided for your wolf. Everyone wanted that soulful connection fate had destined. Wolves relied on instinct. They knew who their mate was long before the human side. They wanted one thing, their true mate. Being at odds with half of yourself did not make for a happy life. That constant internal turmoil was not what any one of them wanted for the rest of their life.

Dash was in agreement with his wolf on mating. No other would do but their true mate. He didn't care how long he had to wait for her. It would happen. When it did happen, it would be the best feeling of his life. For he would know his future would be filled with love, happiness, and contentment.

Chapter 11

Saturn handed out telescopes to those students who wanted one. They were starting their series on planets. With tonight being the harvest moon, she was excited. Before, in the city, she would go up onto the roof to try and catch a glimpse of it. Never could get a good look. Stanley would hound her for doing something stupid. She missed being able to stargaze. There hadn't been much of an opportunity to do what made her soul sing.

She had a backpack packed with snacks and bottles of water. Her telescope was in its case. Shivers ran up her spine, knowing her baby would be out of its case, and put it together that night. Her Celestron edge had been a gift from her parents when she graduated with her degrees. Giggling to herself, if Stanley had known how much it was worth, he probably would have pawned it.

Autumn in Wyoming was different from where she used to live. It got colder at night. Saturn could feel the difference in the air. She loved that it got warm during the day, but as soon as the sunset, it got cooler. Perfect sleeping weather with the windows open, that cool breeze blowing in. Some mornings she was too comfortable in bed that she didn't want to move.

That was a new sensation for her. Married to Stanley, she tried to be up and out of bed before he woke. He was one of those, Look what I have for you, babe. You planning on taking care of it? Let's fuck. It wasn't that she didn't like sex. It was who her partner had been. Her ex was a five-second man. Thrust, thrust, thrust, oh baby, slide into home and done. What was the point? No foreplay. It was all about his pleasure. Made her wonder how he had a mistress.

Saturn was dressed in long underwear under her sweatpants. Jeans were not as comfortable as sweats. She had a long-sleeved t-shirt underneath her hoodie. A jacket tied around her waist if she needed it. Mittens and a hat were stuffed in the backpack. When she watched the sky, finding planets, looking at the moon, she didn't feel the temperature around her. The world around her melted away until she was a part of the universe.

She had hiked the area across the street from her house. It wasn't a bad hike. Saturn was thankful she had done it a few times before carrying her bags. The last time it had taken her thirty minutes or so to get to a nice plateau that would give her a clear view of the sky. There was another flat spot fifteen minutes further up if she felt more adventurous. Depended on how well she could see. Either way, she would be doing something that she loved doing.

Her excitement got the best of her as she hiked. Deciding to go further up, Saturn wanted the best viewing spot she could attain. She was glad she had decided to hike at dusk and not wait until it was completely dark. The thermos of hot coffee in her backpack would taste so good once she got settled. She thought that bringing her sleeping bag was another good idea and a foldable camp chair and blanket. The backpack was on the heavy side but well worth it. If she decided to not hike back down in the dark, she could easily sleep under the stars.

That had been one of her favorite childhood memories. Camping under the stars. No tent, just a sleeping bag with the universe above you. Saturn found peace when she was out in the night air, gazing up into the sky. There had been a few nights when she had been troubled with her marriage to Stanley that she drove out of town, found a spot where she could hike, camp, and look to the sky for answers. It cleared her mind, freed her heart to see what was true.

It had been one of those nights when she had looked to the sky for guidance that she realized it was time to let go. Let go of a dream that her husband would love her unconditionally, cherish, and desire her. Marrying Stanley had been a mistake. Saturn was happy she came to her senses. Don't keep trying to make a bad situation better. He was never going to change. She had changed to attempt to keep him happy. In the end, she had almost lost herself to a man who could have cared less about her.

She shook her head to rid it of the past. There was no room in her life for what was, only what could be. Saturn set up her telescope, taking out her chair, unfolding it. She laid out her sleeping bag. The little lantern that she carried with her set next to her feet. She smiled as she poured herself a cup of coffee. Soon the night sky would be dark. The moon would take center stage. She couldn't wait.

Chapter 12

Over the past month, he heard more about Saturn than any other newcomer to Moonless. Dash was intrigued by this woman who captivated most of his pack. The other teachers who were pack members loved her. She fit right in the community. Parents of children in her classes raved about how well she taught, her kindness to the students. The kids each babbled on about what they had learned. Daily, one of the pups, would come to tell him what the weather was going to be.

He swore fate was working against him. Each time he set off to visit the school, something needed his attention. Mostly it involved Scarlett. Either by herself or an altercation with another female. His betas had stopped trying to intercede. Each time they did, Scarlett cried wolf. Blake didn't like her because she wouldn't go out with him. Jake felt the same way. They were discriminating against her because she was single. Everyone was jealous of her because of her beauty.

As far as Dash was concerned, his wolf agreed with him. Scarlett was not beautiful. Maybe on the outside, but her personality made her ugly. This last time he put out the ultimatum. Either get a job, stop being a bitch, or leave the pack. He was done with the childish drama. The pack females were strong women. They were not going to back down from an insult. A person did not go around telling others how to dress or live their life. Each one was an individual with their own style. Just because you disagreed with them did not mean you needed to point out their flaws. Not one of them was perfect. Scarlett needed to remember that she, too, had flaws.

He prayed tonight didn't have any drama. It was the harvest moon. They would have dinner together as a pack, then go for a run. Dash promised the kids it would be a short run so they could go to the clearing with their telescopes. He was all for that since that was one of his favorite pastimes when he wanted to unwind. His wolf loved the feeling of being under the night sky.

Dinner was enjoyable. Dash had to glare at Scarlett twice. A deep growl had her wolf cowering in submission. The roll of her eyes when a couple of the kids reminded him of his promise had not gone unnoticed. There had been one time he made a mistake with Scarlett. She wanted to hike with him to experience what the stars looked like through a telescope. She was convincing. He hadn't scented her lie. What he considered gazing up at the night sky and what she thought were two different things. She thought it was code for making out, leading to sex. He wanted to look up at the night sky and see what he could see. She had been greatly disappointed.

That hadn't been the last time she had been disappointed. When Dash became the Alpha, Scarlett attempted to move into the packhouse. She quickly found out that no one was going to live there. It was being transformed to function more efficiently. Then she decided to start bossing around other pack members. Complaining that no one listened to her. His reply had been straightforward. She wasn't the Luna, would never be, get over it.

All of them shifted into their wolves. Dash made sure he was leading the little ones. That was one sure-fire way to discourage Scarlett. For someone who wanted to be his mate, she didn't seem to like children or others. He felt pity for whoever was her mate. They took off running. He loved the feel of the air ruffling his fur, his four paws hitting the ground. It had been too long since he had shifted, letting his wolf run free.

Chapter 13

It didn't take long before the pups grew tired of running and wanted to do something else. Dash sent them back to get the telescopes. He was on his way to the clearing when he heard Blake in his head. Alpha, we have a situation. Saturn is at the clearing, so is Scarlett. We will protect Saturn.

Why was he getting the impression that his betas knew something and weren't telling him? His wolf shook out his fur as he ran through the trees. Dash wasn't concerned with Saturn being there. His worry was Scarlett and her temperament. Running faster, approaching the clearing, he shifted to his human self, drawing back the clothing he wore before his wolf had taken over. What greeted him was one of wonderment.

Blake, Jake, and a few other pack members surrounded Scarlett, pushing her further back into the woods. Saturn was oblivious to what was happening around her. Dash stopped to watch as she was slightly bent over looking through her telescope, headphones covering her ears, ass wiggling to the music as she sang along. His wolf repeated one word to him. Mate.

What a beautiful sight. Dash approached her. Tapping her on the shoulder, he said, "Hi. I see you had the same idea I did, along with most of the children in your class. They are on their way with the telescopes you gave them. I'm Dash, by the way."

She jumped when she felt the tap on her shoulder. Slipping off her earphones as she turned, Saturn did not know what they had in the water out this way, but every man she met was ruggedly handsome. This one made her think of a big, cuddly teddy bear. One that would surround you and protect you from the world. She wanted to climb him like a tree, wrapping herself around him until the world around them melted away. "It's a beautiful night to be able to see the moon and planets. The kids are great. They were excited about tonight. Nice to finally meet you, Dash. I'm Saturn."

What he wanted to do was take her in his arms and kiss the hell out of her. He took a step closer to do what his wolf wanted when he heard all the kids bursting through the brush. Dash got pushed back as the children each had to hug their teacher, talking a mile a minute. He didn't know how she kept up with it, but Saturn answered each one of them.

He started to love her at that minute. She stopped to help each one set up their telescopes, taking the time to answer every question, showing them where to look. There was no rush with how she reacted to each child. No grimace came across her lips, never had the smile that she wore when she turned left. Dash knew from the looks of her telescope that it was not a cheap one. He priced them out when he was looking to upgrade his. Her model was one he dreamt about. Even with how advanced hers was, she let the kids look through it. Not afraid they would break it or harm it, she shared her enthusiasm with the pups. She kicked her sleeping bag out of the way to make room for everyone. He was in awe of his mate.

Saturn was having fun with the kids. Sneaking peeks at Dash whenever she could. There was something about him that made her feel protected. Same as she had with Blake, Jake, Mark, and Henry, but this was a little different. With those four, she felt a brotherly connection. Dash was more romantic, primal, and desirable. It had been a long time since she felt a stirring in her girly area. His voice made her nipples harden. That had never happened. She had thought her sex drive had dried up. Good to know it had been dormant, waiting on the right one to reawaken.

Chapter 14

After she let each kid look through her telescope and set theirs up to see what she was looking at, she went over to Dash. He had a nice one, and she was impressed. A handsome, sexy man who liked to gaze up at the sky had her luck finally taken a turn for good. Saturn wasn't going to question it. Fate did some odd things. "Dash, did you want to take a look through mine?"

He had been waiting for this opportunity to get closer to his mate. Dash was not turning her down. "To be honest, I've dreamed about owning a telescope like yours. It would be an honor if you would show me how it works and to see through it."

She felt brazen, taking his hand in hers. Saturn felt the electric zing travel up her arm. It didn't hurt like a static charge, more of a sensual tingle. Her mind wandered a bit, wondering if his touch had that effect on other parts of her body. She explained the controls, keeping her hand on his broad shoulder as he took a look. "Explore a little bit with a clear night like tonight. You may be able to see Mercury or Venus."

Dash moved the scope, zooming in further, scanning the sky until he thought he saw Mercury. It was breathtaking to see one of the planets in their galaxy. He lifted his head, taking a chance to snake his arm around her waist, drawing her closer to him. "Take a look. I think that's Mercury."

Saturn enjoyed having his arm around her. It felt natural for them to be this close. With her ex, she ignored her instincts. That was not happening again. Her instincts were telling her Dash was the one. She didn't know how or why but knew it felt right. Leaning over to look through the lenses, she said, "Yes, that is Mercury."

Before she could say another word, the kids came barreling over to see the planet. Saturn took this opportunity to install some knowledge. "Some important facts about Mercury. One year is eighty-eight days long. It is the smallest planet but the second hottest. Also, it has the most craters and no moons."

The way she talked about the planet, it was easy to feel and see this was one of her passions. Dash knew she liked to bake. He had heard from his betas about her cookies and loaves of bread. She was perfect for him and his wolf. They seemed to like the same things. The way she was with the younger pack members told him how she would be as his Luna. Fate was never wrong.

Saturn moved the scope, trying to find another planet for the kids to view. Venus was usually easy for her to see. It was one of the brighter planets. It was odd, but she felt Dash's presence next to her. She felt as though he was touching her when he wasn't. Saturn was thrilled when she found the tricky planet. Stepping back so that others could take a peek. "This is Venus. A year on Venus equals two hundred and twenty-two earth days. When you look up at the night sky, the moon is the brightest, but the next brightest star is not a star, but the planet Venus. It is also known as the morning and evening star. Venus is the hottest planet in our solar system besides the sun. That is because it does not tilt on its axis. There is no seasonal change. "

He stepped up to look. There were no words to describe what he was looking at. You could see these planets on the web, in textbooks, but to see it through a scope blew your mind. It made you wonder if there was life outside of earth. Were they peering through telescopes at the earth, feeling what he was? To humans, he was a mythical being. Dash had always been a thinker, wondering how things worked and the outcome of a said reaction. According to his dad, that was why he was a good Alpha. He saw life in color, then everything was black and white.

This night was magical in numerous ways. He found his mate. She was intelligent, beautiful, sexy, and kind. Dash got to see planets he had never seen before. It had not been easy to cut the night short. If he had his way, they would have stayed out until the sun rose. The kids' parents called for them. Blake and Jake popped in to escort the little one's home, allowing him to hike down with Saturn. "Kids, it's time to get back home. We can come back and do this again. I'm sure we can ask Saturn to bring her telescope back up here."

She giggled as all the children pleaded with her that they could do this again soon. "I'll check with my parents on a date when maybe we can see other planets. They study them, so they would know. Plus, we can also come out without a telescope to see the constellations. There is more than the Big and Little Dipper."

He helped her pack up her belongings. Dash took her hand in his. "I'll walk you home, Saturn."

Chapter 15

It had taken forever to find out where the bitch had run off to. Stanley was zero help. Heather asked him a few times if he heard from her. His response was always the same. "Why would I want to hear from her? Why do you care? Afraid that I'm cheating on you with her?" She was not concerned with him cheating on her. Keep him sexually happy. Men didn't stray.

Luckily for her, she knew a private investigator that accepted other forms of payment besides cash. She wasn't above using her body to get what she wanted. It worked in both of their favor. No paper trail for either of them. With what Heather was planning on doing to Saturn, no traces of her was the best route to travel.

She told Stanley her mother was ill. The truth was her mother was well and vacationing on a cruise ship for senior singles. Some would say that modern technology was terrible. How everyone was glued to their cell phones had stopped communication between people. She saw it as a godsend. If her mother decided to call her without a landline, it went straight to her cell phone. Stanley was none the wiser.

Today's society did have its pitfalls. It was impossible to fly under an assumed name. She was above taking a nasty bus for those thousands of miles. Driving by herself was not safe. Heather knew she was beautiful. Truck stops were full of men looking to hook up with a beautiful woman. Then there were the hotels on the highway. She didn't trust them if a man were to follow her back to her room and break down the door. In the end, she chose to fly to Wyoming and rent a car.

***

That stupid, tiny human was the Alpha's mate. It was absurd to think of a weak woman standing by his side. Scarlett knew she was supposed to be by Dash's side. She was born a wolf, the same as he was. Their bloodlines were pure. Why taint them with someone who would be a half-breed?

She knew she couldn't get the pack to turn on him or force him to mate with her. They accepted what fate decided. Sometimes fate was wrong. As soon as she was Luna of the pack, things were going to change. The first thing she was changing was the packhouse. It was bigger than where Dash lived. She deserved a vast house with servants. The pack was supposed to wait on the Alpha couple. They were the subordinates.

Scarlett was tired of those around her telling her what she needed to do with her life. Find a job, make herself a home, and mind her own business. That was what males were for. They provided the money while the females spent it. A house was not a home without a male in your bed every night. Who wanted to live alone? She wanted someone to cook and clean for her. As Luna, that would happen in the packhouse. One obstacle stood in her way of achieving her dreams: Saturn.

Since the night of the harvest moon, Scarlett followed Saturn. From a distance, downwind as much as possible. If Dash wasn't around, then Blake, Jake, Mark, or Henry was. She couldn't risk any of them catching her scent. There had been numerous warnings given to her by the Alpha about her attitude towards other pack members. One more violation, and she would be out of the pack. Stalking the mate of the Alpha was a significant violation. She wouldn't be able to charm or talk her way out of that one.

What she needed was someone to do the dirty deed of killing Saturn. Then she could play the comforting friend to Dash. Win him over and become his mate. If his true mate was dead, he would have to take another. For the health of the pack, of course. Scarlett would have to go out of town to find someone. Find a human that would do her bidding. It should be easy enough.

Chapter 16

Since that night that he found her, Dash was making it a point of dating Saturn. He would bring her lunch at school. Take her out to dinner at the diner or meet her at her house to cook for her. He enjoyed the nights that he cooked for her. It was natural the way that they moved around the kitchen together. She never let him do all the cooking.

He found out about her family. How she worked with her parents. Dash realized how much they had in common. He knew she would fit into the pack with ease. Anyone who met her liked her immediately, except for one. He was prepared to deal with Scarlett if she posed a problem. Saturn was his mate. He would kill to protect her.

Dash would feel better if Saturn was already his mate. She would have the protection of having her own wolf. He would also be more at ease if she was living with him. His wolf was on edge. It was more than the contempt that Scarlett was exhibiting. He was concerned regarding that ex-husband of hers.

When she told him about her marriage and divorce, he saw red. His wolf was ready to hunt the asshole down and rip his throat out. Dash had to tell his wolf that they wouldn't have found her without her living through that ordeal. That soothed the furry beast in that aspect but did nothing to calm his uneasiness. His betas and sheriffs were taking turns keeping an eye on his mate. They had been since they met her because they liked her.

She was falling in love with Dash. It was an unconscious feeling. They talked with ease, shared stories from their past, and enjoyed being around one another. He was the first man besides her dad to cook for her. Saturn saw a lot of similarities between her mom and dad in the budding relationship she had with Dash.

Her parents did most activities together. Growing up, if Mom was preparing dinner, then Dad was in the kitchen helping somehow. Cleaning up from dinner was the same. They worked as a team. He enjoyed the same things that she did. Quiet nights sitting outside or watching a movie. Food was meant to be enjoyed. It didn't need to be anything fancy as long as it tasted good. They had taken a couple of long walks through the woods. Both of them liked living a quiet life. Didn't need to go to bars for a good time.

There was a connection developing between them. Saturn could feel it. It was more profound than a shared desire for one another. Their nights started to turn sensual. A soft touch here or there, a kiss that would start innocent and turn steamy. They came close to burning dinner a time or two. When Dash kissed her, she lost all thought. Her body went up in flames. Her panties grew wet. She swore she heard him growl a time or two. That made her body tingle, her nipples pebble. She was ready to take the next step with Dash. It may have been a short period of time since they met one another, but it felt right. She had no hesitation within herself on giving herself fully to him.

He was ready to explain himself to Saturn. Show her his wolf, make her his mate. Dash was in love with her. Time meant nothing when your soul found its other half. He had taken more cold showers since meeting his mate than he had in all of his life. It was about giving her time to fall in love with him. He would give her all the time that she needed, even if his wolf was pushy. First, she needed to know who he really was.

Chapter 17

Part of her plan was to find someone to do the dirty deed. Scarlett was not getting her hands bloody. That would mess up her perfect nails. She had an image to uphold. Dash wouldn't fall in love with her if he could sense her lies. The less that she knew, the better. She had been avoiding him since he found his mate. He was the Alpha. She had to tell him the truth when compelled. It was better for her to keep to herself until that woman was dead.

Scarlett drove out of Moonless, heading west to find a bar. She was on the hunt for a man. Praying that a little sexual activity would seal the deal and she wouldn't be out any cash. As it was, she may have to sell her designer handbags and shoes to raise money for her plan to work. She scoured websites that would gain her the best price. It was not something she wanted to do, but it would be well worth the self-sacrifice in the end.

She pulled into the parking lot of the Firefly. This wasn't her first time at the bar. Scarlett liked this one since there was a hotel next door. Made for an easy hook-up. Striding into the dimly lighted room, stepping up to the bar, she ordered a sour apple martini. Turning on her stool as she was waiting for her drink, she surveyed the area. It was still early, hopefully as the night drew later, more men would stop in for a drink on their way home.

Heather rented a car and reserved a room at a hotel an hour outside of the backward little town where the bitch decided to live. It was an okay hotel, not as lovely as she was used to. The doors opened into the parking lot, no room service or pool. One good aspect was they accepted cash without a credit card. No trail there to tie back to her.

She headed over to the bar next door for a drink, praying they served some kind of food. Heather preferred to have some sort of food in front of her when she drank. Nachos would be good, or some cheesy fries. When she was with Stanley, she ate healthy salads. He hated that his ex-wife didn't take his feelings on how she looked into consideration and ate whatever she pleased.

In her college days, she had dabbled with her sexuality. Threesomes, foursomes, men or women—didn't matter much. If it was enjoyable, pleasurable, then why not indulge? Heather noticed the striking woman as she walked into the bar, deciding to sit next to her. "Hey, gorgeous. Do you know if they serve food here? Care to join me for a snack if they do? Can I buy you a drink?"

Scarlett rolled her eyes. It wasn't until she turned her head that she got confused. This person hitting on her smelled like a female but had characteristics that were male. Were they a crossdresser? She had seen a few of them from time to time in this bar. Some of those men who dressed like a woman looked hot. She would kill for their outfits. They knew how to shop and what the best brands were. "They serve bar food. Nachos, pizza, fries, and burgers. Your accent doesn't sound from around here. In town for something special?"

Heather shrugged. "I'm looking for my boyfriend's ex. When they divorced, she took his keys to the storage unit and his grandmother's rings and refused to mail them back to him. The rings were awarded to him by the courts. Those are supposed to be mine. The bitch moved to Moonless. Ever heard of it?"

Now this woman had her attention. Scarlett would play along with the flirting. There was only one person who moved to Moonless recently, Saturn. She could tell that this woman was lying about her reasons for hunting the bitch down. This was going to work out nicely if her hunch was correct. "I'm actually from Moonless. Let me guess, you are talking about Saturn? Why don't we order some food, more drinks, and move this conversation to a more private table?"

She ordered them a plate of nachos, a pizza, and more drinks. Heather couldn't believe her luck. From the sound of it, this woman didn't like the bitch any more than she did. This was going to be easier than she initially thought. She followed the woman to a secluded table. "You know where Saturn lives? I am looking to retrieve the items with or without her consent. Without would work better, since there could be a nice sum involved for a little bit of assistance."

This had to be one of the best nights she had in a long time. Scarlett was ready to put that mate-stealing bitch in the ground. The sooner, the better. "I believe we can help each other out with this situation. Since she stole my man. We have to act quickly."

As they ate, they hatched up a plan. Heather would ride with Scarlett back to Moonless. They didn't want anyone to get suspicious over out-of-town license plates. She had a shotgun in her trunk that she stole from her father. She knew Saturn had her bed in front of one window. All they had to do was fire through a window, hit their target, and drive off. No one would be the wiser. Tonight, would be the night she got Dash back.

Chapter 18

He waited until the necklace he had designed for Saturn was finished. Dash designed a pendant that had two wolves at the bottom looking up at the night sky. The center was a diamond representing the moon with ruby for Mars, amethyst for Pluto, topaz for Saturn, emerald for Earth, sapphire for Neptune, and black onyx for Mercury. Smaller diamonds surrounded the planets as stars. It wasn't all the planets, but it was a good representation. He hoped she loved it.

They cooked dinner together like they did most nights. Tonight, he set up a blanket and candles in the clearing. Dash thought of it as their spot. It was where his love for Saturn started to grow. He thought it was fitting that he gave her the necklace at their place when he asked her to be his mate. Also gave him plenty of space to shift and catch her if she ran. He didn't think she would, given her love of wolves. Never could tell, though.

She hoped this was the night that they acted on their desire for one another. Saturn was ready to make love to Dash. Their heavy make-out sessions awakened her body to new heights that she never thought existed. He seemed nervous about their night. She could tell that he was an alpha man, one that took charge, took care of others. He let his guard down around her. Made her fall deeper in love with him.

That was one of the many things she loved about Dash. He didn't hide his emotions from her. She heard about Scarlett and her antics. It was sad when a woman would not take no for an answer. Made them seem desperate. Especially when love was not the driving factor. Saturn understood the lure of money with some. Dash could care less how much was in her bank account, the same as she felt about his. Love was about the person, who they were, how they treated others, not about money.

He took her hand as they finished cleaning up the kitchen. "Let's go for a walk, love."

She grabbed her jacket as she followed him out of her home. "I like the sound of that. The sky is clear tonight. Are we going to our spot?"

He chuckled as his wolf nodded. "I love that you think of the clearing as our spot. That is where we are going."

They hiked up the hill. Dash could sense his betas nearby but giving them privacy. He swore he could smell his parents. It wouldn't surprise him much. The pack was waiting for him to take this step. He laughed when they made it to the clearing. The candles were lit. There seemed to be more of them. A couple extra blankets had appeared as well as a covered dish of cupcakes and a thermos filled with something. There was some meddling happening with this night. "I wish I could take all the credit for this, but it wasn't all me. I laid down a blanket and a couple of candles. The rest, I'm guessing, was my parents and other folks from town."

She snuggled closer to him. No one had ever done anything as romantic as this. Saturn felt the tears forming in her eyes. This is what couples in love did for one another. "It doesn't matter what the others did, which is nice. What matters is that you thought to do this for me. It's beautiful, Dash."

He sat down on the blanket, drawing her down to sit in his lap. His wolf was itching to get free. He wanted his mate to see how beautiful he was. Taking the box out of his pocket, he handed it to her. "Saturn, I love you. I have since that first night, then my love for you has grown deeper. Will you be my mate? Being my mate is more than being married. It means we are tied to one another forever. You would be by my side as my Luna, helping run Moonless."

She opened the box, her fingers softly tracing over the stones. Saturn knew what it meant. It was the planets with wolves. Furrowing her brows, she realized he said 'mate'. She had studied enough animals to know their significant other was a mate. Luna was the Alpha's wolf's mate. Wait? Was what she was thinking actually real? Was Dash the Alpha of a wolf pack? Was Moonless the pack? One way to find out. "Dash, are you a werewolf?"

Dash hadn't expected that question. She was smart and picked up on his clues. Damn, she was breathtaking when she figured things out. "Not a werewolf like in myths or movies. More like we have another side to ourselves, which is a wolf. We don't need the full moon to shift into our wolf. It can be done at any time. As my mate, you would get your own wolf. I am the Alpha of the Moonless pack. Would you like to see my wolf? He wants to meet you."

Saturn smiled at him as she leaned closer to place a kiss on his lips. None of what he had said made her feel any different towards him. She knew it had to be hard to tell her about that side of himself. "I would like to meet your wolf."

Chapter 19

He stood up, taking a few steps away from her, letting his wolf come to the forefront of his mind. Dash felt the shift take over. Where he was standing on two legs, he was now on four. Shaking out his fur as he padded closer to her. He was careful to take his time to not scare Saturn. Her actions surprised him. She wrapped her arms around his wolf's neck and nuzzled her face into his fur. This was one of the best moments in his life. Their mate was accepting them.

***

They had made it to the bitch's house. She had every intention of turning the tables on Heather. After she shot up the house, Scarlett planned on shifting and ripping her throat out. Then she could play it off that she had been out running when she heard the gunshots and came to investigate. While she couldn't save the Alpha's mate, she killed the one who brought a threat to the pack. She had a bottle of perfume in the center console. All she had to do was spray the inside of her car with it. The floral scent should throw off whoever. That would redeem her in Dash's eyes. He would be grateful.

She planned on shooting up the house before turning the gun on Scarlett. Heather wasn't stupid. The less who knew she was involved, the better. There was no way she was sharing any of the insurance money with anyone. This woman was a means to an end. She had gloves on as she took the shotgun from the trunk. It wouldn't be her fingerprints on the weapon or the shells. One snag was, she was going to steal her car to get back to the hotel. After that, she was checking out and hitting the road back to the airport.

Scarlett showed her which window was which. Heather took aim at the bedroom window, shooting it out before reloading. Shooting a few more rounds, aiming lower, praying the bitch was in bed with her head blown off. To be on the safe side, she went around to the back, fired a few rounds through the kitchen window, then the front window. There was no way Saturn could have survived.

As soon as all the windows had been shot out, Scarlett shifted into her wolf. Charging at Heather, ready to rip her throat out, when she turned the shotgun on her. Scarlett felt the first shot hit her shoulder. She fell to the ground as her leg gave out. This was not how her plan was supposed to go. She was supposed to be the victor, not this stupid human. In the next shot, she felt her body go limp. She gasped one last breath before she closed her eyes.

Seeing the woman turn into a wolf had been horrific. To think those creatures lived among them, looking normal. Heather had done humanity a favor by putting a bullet between her eyes. The problem was that there was a wolf, not a human, to pin the crime on. How could she leave the gun between that thing's paws? It didn't fit into her plan. It was desolate where the bitch was living. This gave her time to think. If she put the gun back in Scarlett's trunk, drove back to the bar when the car was found. The authorities would look for that woman as the shooter. Heather knew she was dead. They would never find her. Actually, that worked better.

Chapter 20

She enjoyed the feel of his fur between her fingers. It was so soft, not stiff or wiry like she thought it would be. Saturn felt him get stiff in her embrace and heard the deep guttural growl. On instinct, she moved back, not that she was afraid of him, but something had changed. That was when she heard the echo of gunshots. "Are you in danger, love? Is someone out there hunting? What do I need to do?"

Dammit, motherfucking hell, why now? He was thankful he had decided to bring his mate up to the clearing. If they stayed at her house, had been in bed becoming mates, she would be dead. Someone was going to die tonight, and it was not his Saturn. Mark and Henry had one suspect. The other was dead. Linking to his betas, he sent, Come take care of my mate. Do not let anything happen to her.

Before she could utter a single syllable, Dash headed down the hill while Blake and Jake emerged from the forest. She already figured out that they were wolves, along with the rest of the town. Mayor, Alpha, kind of the same thing. Didn't take a rocket scientist to figure that one out. Squaring off towards the two men, her hands on her hips. "Where did he go? Take me to him. Now!"

They looked at one another. Their Alpha said to take care of her, not let anything harm her. Blake knew the person was disarmed. Mark and Henry had her. She couldn't hurt Saturn if they took her to Dash. Their wolves were cowering, listening to her as they recognized her as their Luna. "We will take you. It was your house that was shot up. Someone was trying to kill you, Saturn. Two someone's, to be exact. "

That made her stop and think. Who would try to kill her? Saturn was baffled by these facts. "Besides the fact I want to show Dash I will be by his side no matter what he is facing, I want to see who wants me dead. Let's go."

Blake trailed behind her while Jake was in front. He felt Dire and Tala flank them out of sight on the sides. His wolf was overjoyed to hear she wasn't shrinking back from what had happened. Their Alpha had a strong-willed female for a mate. He chuckled as she pushed past Jake to run over to Dash. This was their Luna.

She ran over to Dash, taking his hand in hers. Saturn gave him a smile when their eyes met. Her attention was drawn to the woman that was being held. "You, it was you who wanted me dead. Why? You wanted my husband. I gave him to you. What more is there?"

Dash was astounded that his mate knew this woman. The other one in this plot to kill Saturn had been Scarlett. He knew her wolf by sight and scent. How the two of these females had met up was what he wanted to know. He also wanted to know the reason from this woman. "Answer her!"

Heather decided to go with the waterworks. Tears had gotten her out of speeding tickets. It would work in this instance. "It wasn't me who wanted you dead; it was that wolf. I shot it trying to save my own life. Would you believe that wolf was a woman? I met her down the road as I was walking to find you. You left some items back at the condo when you moved out. I wanted to return them to you."

There was a round of bullshit that could be heard from all in attendance. Dash decided to clarify the situation a little better for this woman. "First, I can smell your lies. Second, yes, I am aware that the wolf used to be a female. Thirdly, I believe it was a plot between the two of you, but one turned on the other. Fourthly, you stink of gunpowder, which means it was you that held the shotgun and fired it. Care to try again?"

There was always money. No one could turn that down. Heather prayed she could talk herself out of this situation with the promise of a big payoff. Once she was back home, she could change her name and appearance. No one would be the wiser. "I did shoot the gun, but it was because I feared for my life. Scarlett kidnapped me. She had this all planned out. It was supposed to be me that died. I can pay you whatever sum you want to be able to leave here. I won't say a word about what I saw. Think about it. Name a number."

Saturn rolled her eyes. Even she knew Heather was full of shit, and she didn't have an enhanced sense of smell. "That's bullshit. You were yelling at me at the courthouse because the judge didn't award Stanley alimony. If I had to guess, this has to do with money. My second guess was you found the old life insurance policy and thought it was still enforced, leaving Stanley all the money if I died. Stupid, stupid, stupid— should have called the company. That was changed before the divorce was final."

She lunged at Saturn, ready to claw her eyes out with her fingernails. Her plan was flawless. Heather couldn't control her anger anymore. "If you weren't such a shrew bitch then I wouldn't be out in some hole in the wall town in the middle of fucking nowhere! Stanley was an idiot. He should have stayed married to you to siphon off all the money. How did you end up with this hot guy? Let me guess, he is loaded too. Figures it's the ugly ones that get the rich, hot men. You can't keep me here. I know my rights. Either charge me with the crime or let me go."

It was his turn to chuckle. This woman had no clue what she was facing. Dash knew what needed to be done. "As Alpha of the Moonless pack, you attempted to bring deadly harm to my mate. No threat against the ruling couple goes unpunished. Scarlett broke a cardinal rule by shifting in front of a human. By doing so, she put everyone at risk. No one can know our secret. Your sentence is death."

Chapter 21

She wasn't shocked by his declaration. In her heart and soul, she knew he was protecting not only her but also the pack. Those little children she saw every day at school who were so excited about seeing the stars would be in danger. The others she came to think of as friends could be hurt for being who they were. Saturn squeezed Dash's hand. "It must be done."

He was afraid what he was about to do next would scare his mate away. Once again, she surprised him by supporting his decision. Dash was in awe of Saturn. Her strength, determination, and beauty were why he was so deeply in love with her. She was his Luna. Turning to draw her into his arms, his lips found hers. "We have some unfinished business, love, when this is all over. You might wish to close your eyes or turn around. It will not be pretty. My wolf has to feel her blood coat his fur to know that the threat to you is gone."

Saturn kissed him back, pouring all the love that she felt for him into that kiss. "Seeing your wolf kill her will not make me afraid of him. He is a part of you. I love you, Dash, all of you. And to answer your earlier question. Yes, I will be your mate."

Dash kissed her one last time before he stepped away to shift into his wolf. He was floating on cloud nine with her agreeing to be his mate. His wolf was ready to get this over with, pushing to the forefront, making the shift happen. He let a deep, menacing snarl, baring his teeth as he approached Heather.

She couldn't help the giggles that escaped. It was amusing. For someone who had tried to kill her, attempted to bully her for money, blamed her for having to cut back on expenses, Heather was not talking shit now. In fact, she had pissed herself. Saturn found it ironic. With the breeze kicking up, if the smell reaching her was any indication, she had also shit her pants. This night was one she would never forget.

He let out a series of howls to signal that the Alpha was serving justice to one who tried to bring harm to the pack. Mark and Henry had stepped back from the woman. They couldn't hold her for justice to be served. It wouldn't be a fair fight, but the restraints were gone. His wolf lunged for her throat. She attempted to turn, bring her arms up to block the attack. None of it worked. He maneuvered his body mid-air to avoid all obstacles. Dash felt his teeth sink into the soft tissue of her neck.

This was not how this night or trip was supposed to go. She hadn't murdered Saturn. Her plan failed, so why was this happening to her? Who would miss her? Stanley sure as hell wouldn't. Her being gone meant he was free. Heather thought for a moment where she had gone wrong. She deserved to have the hot, sexy guy, not have to work, be waited on like she was a queen. Not having a wolf's teeth sinking into her neck. This was not justice. She had the God-given right to a fair trial with a jury of her peers. Her constitutional rights were being violated.

He closed his jaws around her neck, tasting her blood as it ran across his tongue. Dash kept his hold tight until she stopped moving, her blood coating his fur and the ground. His wolf shook his head, ripping her throat to shreds. This woman was no longer a threat as he spat out her flesh. He turned, giving his mate a bloody, lupine grin.

She usually wasn't a violent person. Except in this instance, Saturn felt like justice had been served. It was the only option for the situation. The pack did not follow the same rules as humans did, is what she learned. It made sense. They had a secret that needed to be kept. She shook her head at Dash. His wolf had a dangerous side but also a fun side. "You need a shower."

He stalked closer to her, rubbing his side against her legs. He nodded to her to follow him. Her house was shot up. He was not going to let her inside until it was cleaned up. She agreed to be his mate. He was taking her home to their home.

Chapter 22

She followed Dash through the woods. Shocked at how many wolves were roaming around. Saturn didn't know who was who, but they gave them a wide berth. She wondered if it was because he was the Alpha or he was covered in blood. This was a new world opening up to her. Where she would be loved for who she was. A relationship where they enjoyed the same things, talked for hours, time spent together was magical. She had dreamed about this. Now it was becoming a reality.

Not quite how he hoped this night was going to go. Even with the interruptions, hiccups with their plans, his mate was by his side. She had not run scared with any of the revelations. Dash couldn't love her any more than he did at that moment. It was taking forever to get back to his cabin. He was trying to keep both sides of himself calm. This was the first night of the rest of their lives.

She opened the door to his home. Someone brought all the candles from the clearing and set them around his house leading to the bedroom. The cupcakes sat on the counter. Her necklace in the box sat next to them. Saturn wasn't sure how she felt about the entire pack knowing what they were planning on doing together. The closeness of the pack was not something she was used to. Her mind was blown at the thoughtfulness of them. How they thought of her and Dash was special.

He shifted once the door closed behind him. Not taking his human form with any clothes on. What was the point? He planned on removing them rather quickly. Dash took her hand in his. "Don't overthink it, love. They wanted to make sure that our night wasn't ruined. The pack is family. Now, how about that shower?"

Saturn let go of his hand to step in front of him. She took steps towards what she guessed was the bedroom, praying that was where the bathroom was. Either way, she planned on teasing him. They would end up in the bathroom one way or another. Hooking her fingers in the hem of her shirt, she lifted it up and over her head. She smiled at Dash as she unbuttoned her jeans, lowering the zipper, kicking off her shoes as she shimmied her hips, letting the material slide down her legs.

Holy hell, seeing her take off her clothes for him was one of the sexiest things he had ever witnessed. The more of his mate that was revealed for his eyes only drew growls rumbling through his chest. Dash wanted to reach out and pull her into his arms. He wouldn't touch her with blood drying on himself. When her bra fell to the floor, so did his jaw. Being in love with the person you were with made a hell of a difference. This was not fucking between them. What they were going to share was on a completely different level.

She gave him a soft smile. Her body was aching in places that she never knew could feel that way. When he had shifted, and she got her first look at him naked, her body had heated. She had seen him without his shirt before now, and ran her hands across his chest. Yet seeing it all tied together was the sexiest, most erotic thing she ever witnessed or felt. She threw her panties at his head before running off to the bathroom.

Her scent was intoxicating to his wolf. He stalked after her into the bathroom. Dash stepped under the cool spray, waiting until the water had warmed before drawing her flush against him. His lips found hers, a hungry kiss between them with the promise of what was to come. He was finding a new love of sharing showers. It had never been an activity that interested him until Saturn.

Saturn grabbed the soap, washing the blood off Dash. She wanted all that happened that night to be gone. With the blood washing down the drain, so did the attempt on her life, her past, his past. They were coming to one another as who they were. No one else could come between them. As she watched the soap suds wash off his body, she demanded, "Make me your mate, Dash."

Chapter 23

He turned off the water, grabbed a towel, drying her off. Dash picked her up in his arms, kissing her tenderly. Carrying her to the bedroom, laying her across the bed. His hands caressed up her legs as he parted them. Her scent had been driving him crazy each time they were together. He needed to know if she tasted like a strawberry dipped in rich milk chocolate.

Setting between her thighs, he inhaled deeply, letting her scent wrap around him. Dash nuzzled his nose against the folds of her pussy, placing kisses along her skin before he took that first taste as his tongue swiped through her wet folds. He found what he had been craving all these years. Saturn was his new addiction, one he planned on indulging in as often as he could. He circled her clit, teasing her, driving up her pleasure as high as possible.

Wow, that was all that she could think. Saturn never thought that having a man between her legs could feel this damn good. She was feeling sensations that were unknown to her. It felt as though he was touching her entire body. Her hips followed his tongue, needing something more, but she was unsure what that was until her body shattered. She was riding out wave after wave of pure pleasure. Her legs were shaking, her hands balled up in his hair as she moaned out his name in gasps of air.

He kissed up her body as his hip settled between her thighs. Dash loved hearing her come undone. It was sounds he planned on hearing nightly for the rest of his life. He moved her legs to his waist, sliding his cock through her silken folds. If being in her arms, their lips touching as he was balls deep inside of Saturn wasn't heaven, then he didn't know what else was. He felt as though he had come home after a long, exhausting journey. She was his world.

All these years, she thought something was wrong with her when it came to sex. It wasn't her; it was who she was with. They were what was wrong. Saturn felt her orgasm flaring to life again with each stroke. She wrapped her legs around him, angling her hips to take him deeper, earning her a growl from Dash. His growls made her body tingle and her heart race. She loved hearing the noises he made, how he felt against her body, inside her body.

Dash couldn't hold back. With how she was moving with him, he slid his arms underneath her shoulders, lifting her closer to him. As he did that, his cock slid deeper into her slick channel. With each stroke, her clit slid against his skin. He felt her grow wetter, knowing her orgasm was fast approaching, the same as his was. Kissing his way from her lips to her shoulder, he bit down, and his canines pierced her flesh as his orgasm raced through his body. His wolf peered out through his eyes as they made Saturn their mate.

Her orgasm took on new heights when he bit her. Saturn was soaring higher than she ever had. Her body felt like it was floating on the softest clouds, surrounded by pure love. She held onto him for dear life, sure that she would float away as her body calmed. "I love you, my mate."

He rolled, taking her with him until she was lying on his chest. This was their beginning. Dash knew the completeness of having a mate. His soul had found its other half; his heart was overflowing with love and devotion. "I love you, mate."

Chapter 24

They napped, waking in each other's arms, desire flaring for one another. Saturn got to tease him with her mouth on a couple of occasions. Sometimes he let her finish what she started by licking his cock. Other times he would grab her, moving her until he was balls deep inside of her. Each time, however, they started, they finished together. Falling into a breathless heap in each other's arms.

When they had awakened the next day, it was already late afternoon. She felt like a well-loved female. Somewhere, somehow, her house had been packed up and delivered to his house. Some of the boxes were inside, while others were in the garage. She was thankful to whomever thought to do this for them. Sitting on the counter were dishes of bacon, scrambled eggs, and pancakes. Being a part of a wolf pack was like nothing she had ever experienced.

Over the next couple of weeks, they fell into a nice routine. Dash went about his day handling pack or town issues while she went off to teach her classes. The pack accepted his mate with open, welcoming arms. They were all watching her, waiting for her wolf to make an appearance. What he enjoyed the most was falling asleep with her in his arms and waking to have her be the first person he saw as he opened his eyes.

They had a small mating ceremony. It had been a surprise for both of them. Her new in-laws planned it all out. Saturn was honored to be introduced as the Luna of the pack. She noticed some of those she had met before meeting Dash were more relaxed around her now. It made sense. They were used to referring to him as Alpha and around her before censoring what they said. That wasn't easy for some.

She was trying to work out how to break the news to her parents. To them, they were married. It was sudden. Saturn wasn't sure how they would react. She prayed they liked Dash. That was the first time she heard the little voice in her head. They will like our mate. How could they not? Once they meet him, it will all work out. Trust yourself and him.

He remembered the call from Saturn. She hadn't been frantic or more concerned. Dash knew what was happening when she told him she was hearing voices in her head. He had been going over local police reports. They put Heather's body in the forest far from pack land with the shotgun lying next to her and the wolf body of Scarlett. All reports coming in was she was attacked by a pack of wild wolves. The pack needed to be careful for the time being when they shifted and went for a run. Some people got vigilant when they heard news stories and took matters into their own hands.

Dash raced home. Finding his beautiful mate in the kitchen staring out the window. "Hey, love. You are not going crazy. That voice is your wolf. Talk to her, listen to her. Do you feel ready to shift?"

Saturn turned from the window, going over to her mate. Wrapping her arms around his waist as she laid her head on his chest. "I feel edgy. Like I need to run or stretch. Almost like I could crawl out of my skin. I could smell you through the open window. It's a lot to comprehend at once."

He held her tightly. "It can be overwhelming. Take it slowly. Those feelings are your wolf wanting to be free. Your body has changed. Not only is your smell enhanced, so is your hearing and eyesight. Do you want to try to become your wolf?"

She took a deep breath. "Let's try. What do I do?"

Chapter 25

He took her hand in his as he led her outside. "Let your wolf come to the forefront of your mind. Envision her, don't fight the change. Let it flow through your body. Deep breaths, be relaxed. Give it a try, love. I know you can do it."

She listened to what he said. Finding her wolf in her mind, she was beautiful. Saturn took deep breaths like Dash told her to do, closing her eyes as she let her body relax. It felt weird. Didn't hurt, slight pulling and tugging. It seemed like hours when it was seconds that had passed. When she opened her eyes, the world was crisper. Her feet were replaced with paws. She could smell a chipmunk that was five trees over running under a bush.

Dash waited until she made the shift before he shifted to his wolf. *You are beautiful, love. We can communicate through our minds in this form. Think of our connection, and I will hear you.*

This day was full of shocking firsts. First her wolf, and now she could talk to her mate through her mind. *I can hear you. This is amazing, love. Can we run?*

He chuckled. Of course, we can go for a run.

They ran for about an hour before she got tired. Remembering what Dash had said, she envisioned her human self shifting back. Her handsome, sexy mate decided they needed a nap after their run. The nap started with a full body massage, ending with them making love. Saturn was in awe of all the changes that took place since that night of the harvest moon. Forever would that be her favorite spot and time of year. Fate had written in the stars of their finding one another, a true love that would survive anything that life could throw at them.

Dash always had a love of the night sky. It had never made sense to him until that fated night. The other half of his soul that would complete him had been waiting for him to find her. She became his world. It was written in the stars that he would find his mate under the night sky.

The End

About the Author

Prometheus is the mother of two boys, 19 and 26. As well as a loving wife to her husband of 31 years. She lives in northern Illinois with her family, two cats, pet bunny, Fred and a puppy, Bear. An avid Chicago Bears football fan regardless of how bad they play. But differs from the rest of the family in regards to baseball. They are Cub fans while she is a Brewers fan.

For years, Prometheus has had stories floating around in her head when she finally decided to put them to paper. Following a long-held dream of being an author. Bringing the crazy muses that she had to life, sharing them with everyone else.

Besides her love for her family and friends, coffee is her biggest love and addiction. The summer will find her at the beach or waterpark, soaking up those beautiful rays of sunshine. She finds cooking to be very relaxing, experimenting with new recipes. Crafting is one of her other ways to relax and unwind. Pink and sparkly is her signature.

Follow her on Facebook to see what she is up too and for announcements.

facebook.com/prometheus.susan.1

Other Titles by Prometheus Susan

Inked

Through the years Clayton has seen changes in society and the tattoo world. He has built his shop, Inked, to be a sought-out place for both humans and the supernatural. One thing that has eluded him all these years, the true love of a mate.

Echo set out on her own after her parents disowned her. Training to be a tattoo artist she witnesses a horrific crime. With one attempt on her life, not waiting for another, she disappears. Her journey to escape with her life leads her to Inked.

Is Echo the one that Clayton has been searching for all these years?

Can Clayton save her when danger comes calling?

Will Inked be their saving grace?

Harper

Harper grew up being teased and ridiculed for his appearance. Only by breaking free from his pack does he hope to find where he truly belongs. With his brother and sister by his side, the trio hit the open road, doing whatever it takes to survive.

Ember fell for the lies of a con man and lost everything. With little more than the shirt on her back, she sets off on a cross-country voyage in search of a fresh start.

Both of their path's lead to Midnight, Colorado.

Harper never believed he would find his mate who would accept him. But being near Ember awakens a side of him that refuses to be ignored. While she's never seen her new boss, Ember is mystified by how the sound of his voice causes her body to quake with an undeniable need. Can his desire for Ember coax Harper from the shadows? Or will the pasts they're both desperate to outrun ruin their chance at a blissful future?

Her Ghostly Savior

There is no pain like losing a child. That is something Blaze knows all too well. It explains why instead of celebrating the first birthday, she's sitting in a cemetery with balloons holding her grief when she wants nothing more than to be holding her son.

She should share her grief with her husband, Dominic. But that's hard to do when deep down, she can't help but think he had something to do with their son's death in the first place. The only comfort she can find is in a ghost buried near her sweet boy.

The more Blaze and Dominic's marriage dissolves, the harder her gut tells her something isn't right. One trip to a pawn shop with a piece of jewelry he gave her and her entire life as she knew it unravels. Dominic is anything but what he seems, and those gifts aren't gifts at all...

They're trophies.

Lucas has to crossover. That doesn't stop him from watching over Blaze and guarding her against a monster she doesn't know is right on her doorstep.

But when her husband comes for her life, Lucas won't even let the supernatural veil separating them stop him from making sure Blaze remains unharmed.

And acts of love like that certainly have the power to defy even fate.